If Big can...

I can...

D1350216

Beth Shoshan & Petra Brown

meadowside
CHILDREN'S BOOKS

If Big can run...
... then I can run

(Though not as quick,
I'm only small)

If Big can jump…
… then I can jump

(And Big leaps long,
long, long away)

If Big can swing...
... then I can swing

(As Big swings
high into the sky,
I'll get there too,
one day, I'm sure)

If Big can climb…
… then I can climb

(It's just I have to take my time to get to all the places Big can climb to with one stretch)

If Big can see...
... then I can saw

(Up, up I go, into the air.
I never thought I'd get so high,
but now that Big is on the ground
how will I get down?)

If Big can play...

... then I can play

(Deep in the sand Big digs a hole...

...but if I fell in I'd be stuck and then I'd have to
yell and shout for Big to come and pull me out)

But what if Big
can't get in places
only I can squeeze inside?

I'd find the treasures,

Rule the roost!

Be number one...

And Big would know
I'm having fun.

If Big could only see…

...how great it is
inside my den and all
the games I like to play
on oceans round the world
and spaceships in the sky.

Here I can
swing into
the air!

Running quick
and leaping long

and stretch to climb
and soaring high
into the air
and digging deep...

...but Big's not there...

...I'm all alone...

...and that's no fun,

so...

Whatever Big can ...

and whatever I can ...

We can...

...together!

For Danny, Beth, Mimi and Joseph

B.S.

For Callum & Iain

P.B.

First published in 2006
by Meadowside Children's Books
185 Fleet Street
London EC4A 2HS

Text Beth Shoshan
Illustrations © Petra Brown 2006

The right of Petra Brown to be
identified as the illustrator has been
asserted by her in accordance with
the Copyright, Designs and
Patents Act, 1988

A CIP catalogue record for this book
is available from the British Library
Printed in China

ISBN 10 pbk 1-84539-206-X
ISBN 13 pbk 978-1-84539-206-2

ISBN 10 hbk 1-84539-207-8
ISBN 13 hbk 978-1-84539-207-9

10 9 8 7 6 5 4 3 2